Forth

THE
YOUNG·MERLIN·TRILOGY
BOOK THREE

MERLIN

JANE YOLEN

SCHOLASTIC INC.

New York Toronto London Auckland Sydney

For Karen Weller-Watson
who has her own magic

ISBN 0-590-37119-3

Copyright © 1997 by Jane Yolen. All rights reserved.
Published by Scholastic Inc., 555 Broadway, New York, NY 10012, by arrangement with Harcourt Brace & Company.
SCHOLASTIC, APPLE, and associated logos are trademarks and/or registered trademarks of Scholastic Inc.

12 11 10 9 8 7 6 5 4 3 2   8 9/9 0 1 2 3/0

Printed in the U.S.A.   40

First Scholastic printing, September 1998

Text set in Fairfield Medium
Designed by Kaelin Chappell

CONTENTS

Merlin:

The smallest British falcon or hawk,
its wingbeats are powerful and,
despite its size, it seldom fails of its prey.

Dark.

Night.

"It is your turn, Green Man. Set down your cards."

"I have you beaten, little bear. I hold a ten and a face."

"You have cheated."

"I never cheat."

"Except when it pleases you."

"You do not believe me, child?"

"I believe you have a ten and a face. But of what suit? Flowers? Game birds? Or the wild men of the woods? If they do not match, Green Man, I will beat you yet."

"You think too much on winning. On losing. Child, this is a game."

"I like games, Green Man. I am good at them."

"Being good at games should not be your only goal. You must think on other things. There is more to becoming an adult than games."

"Then I do not wish to become an adult. I wish to remain a child and play games. I am good at them."

"Such cannot be. The world grows old, and we with it. All life turns on the great wheel: dark to light to dark again."

"Can you not change that, magic maker?"

"Even I cannot."

"Then what will be left of childhood when we are grown old and gone?"

"Dreams are left, child. Dreams."

"I do not want to be someone else's dream, Green Man. I mean to stay awake."

Light.

Day.

1. FLIGHT

PURSUED BY DREAMS, THE BOY FLED FROM the town. They were not his dreams; they were the town's dreams, rough and hot and angry and full of blood.

He squirmed through a bolt-hole in the stone walls, a hole big enough for a badger or fox. Though twelve years old, he was a small boy and he just managed to fit. Sliding down the grassy embankment, he kept an eye out for the green wagon in which his family—or at least all the family he could claim—had left the town hours earlier.

But as it was night, he somehow got on the

wrong path, and he did not come upon any sign of them. Not the wagon which—even in the dark—would have been unmistakable as it was painted and shaped to look like a castle on wheels. Nor the man who claimed to be his father but was not. Nor the woman who made no such claims. Nor the mules who pulled, nor the horse and cow.

He was on his own. He was alone.

Everything, he thought wildly, *everything conspires to keep me on my lone.* By this he meant he could not go back into the town because of the dreams and because the lord of the town, Duke Vortigern, had told him to go. And because the Duke's own spy, a man named Fowler, hated him and would make him a prisoner if he could. And Fowler's even fouler dog knew his scent and would savage him on command.

And by this the boy also meant that the man in the wagon, Ambrosius, feared the boy's powers, and his woman agreed. They had run not from the Duke's anger but from their own fear.

"I shall have to go into the woods," the boy told himself.

The woods did not frighten him. The entire year he was eight, he had lived abandoned in the forest by himself. He had lived as a wild boy, a *wodewose*, without clothing, without warm food, or bedding, or the comfort of story or song. Without words. Without memory. But he had survived it till tamed by Master Robin, a falconer, and in Master Robin's house given a name and a history.

Surely, he thought, *I can do at twelve what I did at eight.*

But it was the middle of the night, and a forest—even one you know—can be a fearsome place. So he picked out a tree not too deep into the woods, an oak with a tall, ragged crown which he could just make out against the starry sky. It was a sturdy tree, its trunk wider than he could comfortably span with his arms, with a ridged bark that made it easy to climb.

He settled into the V-shaped crotch of the tree, some ten feet off the ground, certain he would be safe there from fox and wolf. Then, pulling his knees up to his chest, he slept.

And dreamed.

He dreamed about a bear in the forest. A bear

with a gold coronet on its head. A bear that walked upright, like a man.

A bear!

In his dream he crossed his fingers, an old trick of his that forced him to wake. Shivering in the dark, he drew his legs up even closer. He had found over the years that his dreams had an uncanny way of coming true, but on the slant. A bear—even slantwise—was a danger. It had teeth and claws. It could climb a tree.

But the bear in his dream had not seemed particularly menacing. It had not even been more than a cub. Besides, the dream was an old one he had had before, and he had yet to see a bear when he was awake, except for one old ratty creature leashed to a traveler that danced to the sad pipings of a flute at the fair. So settling deeper into the curve of the trunk, he slept again.

This time he did not dream.

Birdsong woke him, a blend of thrush and willow tit and the harsh *kraah kraah* of the hoodie crow. His legs were cramped, his shoulders aching, but he was alive. And it was day.

He put his head back and sang:

In the woods, in the woods,
My dear-i-o,
Where the birds, the birds sing
Cheer-i-o . . .

It was all he could remember of a song that Viviane, the woman in the green wagon, had sung once. But even so it gave him heart. He jumped down from the tree, found a stream, and washed his hands and face in the cold water. It was a habit left over from his first family, Master Robin's family.

Thinking about them made him think as well of the man Fowler and his dog who might at any moment be on his trail. Fowler was not the kind of man who slept late or gave up easily.

It should have made the boy afraid, but for some reason it did not. He began singing again as he struck off even more deeply into the woods.

2. FISHING

THE DEEPER HE WENT INTO THE WOODS, the more there were shadows. Overhead, the interlaced branches made a kind of roof that the sun only occasionally broke through. Ahead of him a red butterfly flitted over fallen leaves, settling at last on a patch of ivy. By the side of the path, bittersweet berries were already half changed from green to scarlet and the flooring of bracken was an autumnal copper brown. He liked the sound his feet made as he walked, a soft crunching.

Turning his face toward the yellowing tree roof, he drew in a deep breath. He should have been worried about where his next meal would come from or that Fowler would find him. He should have worried about the dream bear. But somehow here, in the heart of the woods, he felt secure.

Just then he heard the nearby sound of water over stone. Following the sound he came to a small river winding between willows. There was a large grey rock half in and half out of the water and he sat upon it to rest. It was smooth and cool; he liked the feel of it. When he leaned over to look into the water, he was startled by a silvery flash.

Fish, his conscious mind told him. But as he continued staring at its sinuous movement, he became mesmerized, and suddenly he found himself *in* the water, swimming by the fish's side. Overhead, light filtered through the river's ceiling in a shower of golden shards.

The boy swam nose to tail with the trout, following it into deeper and deeper waters where the sunlight could not penetrate. Yet, oddly, he could still see clearly in the blue-green of the river morning.

He did not question that he could breathe

under the water; indeed it seemed as natural to him as breathing air.

Little tendrils of plants, like the touch of soft fingers, brushed by him. Smaller fish darted at the edges of his sight. Then nose to tail, he and the trout traveled even further down into the depths of the darkening pool.

The trout was thick along its back and covered with a shimmer of silver marked with black spots and crosses, like a shield. As it swam, it browsed on tiny shrimp, a moveable feast. Then, suddenly, it turned and stared at him with one bold eye.

"Do not rise to the lure, lad," it said in a voice surprisingly chesty and deep. Bubbles fizzed from its mouth like punctuation. Then it was gone in a flurry of waves, so fast the boy could not follow. He blinked, and once more found himself sitting upon the rock, completely dry.

"That was not exactly a dream," he whispered to himself. But he knew it was not exactly real either. Still, the shards of filtered light through water, the silver back of the trout, its resonant voice had seemed all too true.

"Do not rise to the lure," he repeated quietly, glancing around at the forest. But seeing nothing that looked the least like a lure, he stood, brushed himself off, and headed deeper into the woods.

3. THE PACK

HE PUZZLED OVER HIS ADVENTURE WITH the trout for hours as he walked, but could come to no understanding of it. And while he was puzzling, he paid slight attention to where he was going. Soon he left the small deer trail he had been following and somehow found himself pushing through briars and clambering over fallen logs.

It was midway through the day when he realized that he was not only hungry, he was terribly lost.

Now the woods were dark and filled, unaccountably, with large gullies lined with ash and spindletree and the spikey gorse leaves. Nettles seemed to fence in every new path he chose, as if the woods itself wanted him to go in one direction and one direction only.

By the time he emerged on the other side of one particular ravine, he was soaking wet, part perspiration, part rain, for a fine mist had formed around the ravine's edge, showering down on anything in it. The mist obscured how far he had to climb, how far he had already come.

When he finally crested through the mist, he found himself on a flat piece of land in which grass—such a deep green it looked like an ocean—spread out as far as he could see.

He laughed out loud. If he had been younger, he might have believed he had discovered the land of fairies, for everything seemed jewel-like and perfect. There were blossoms everywhere, as if autumn had been banished from this land and only summer remained. The place was patchworked with pink stitchwort and rosebay willow herb, yellow spikes of agrimony, and blue and purple thistles. Over all was the buzz of summer insects, broad-bodied dragonflies and the long-legged crane fly. He waded through the grass and flowers, the sweet, soft smell almost making him light-headed. Then the sun broke through and everything shimmered as though touched by a magician's wand.

"This . . . this . . . this . . ." he whispered wildly, intoxicated by it all. A cuckoo called out to him and, in his joy, he answered it back.

His voice echoed over and over and, with it, came another sound: the baying of a hound.

Fowler, came his immediate thought, *and his awful dog.* Could they have tracked him so easily and so far?

But then a second and a third hound's voice joined in and he knew the truth of it. There was a pack of wild dogs on his trail and here he was, stuck in the middle of a meadow with no idea in which direction safety lay. Even at eight, he would not have become so beguiled as to forget all danger and stray from the safety of the trees.

He forced himself to remain calm. "Do not," he whispered, "rise to the lure." Turning carefully about, he noted that the closest line of trees lay ahead of him rather than behind. Without another thought, he began to plunge through the high grass toward them.

What had seemed so beautiful and jewel-like moments before now proved stubborn and treacherous. He could make little time through the grass, and the sound of the dogs' bellings seemed closer and closer with each difficult step. But the cries only forced him into greater effort; he swam agonizingly, through the pinks and yellows and purples and blues that topped the green waves.

He was about twenty steps away from the safety of the trees when he heard the dogs close at his heels, no longer baying but snarling. Not being the kind of lad to give up, he kept on running, his breath coming in shorter and shorter gasps, an awful red-hot ache in his chest.

And then something burst through the grass in front of him, something shaggy and hairy and big as a bear. It reached out and grabbed him up, and though he had not the breath to scream, he screamed.

4. CREATURE

THE CREATURE TOOK FIVE STEPS, NO more, and leaped up into an old oak, the boy now snugged under its arm. Behind it, the dogs were snarling and yelping in equal measure, but they were too late. The creature was already into the tree, scrambling upward with such quickness, it reached the third branching of the tree trunk before the pack had ringed the oak below.

All the while the boy kept screaming, a high, horrible sound that he had not known he could make. At each scream, the dogs set up an echoing wail.

The creature set the boy down next to its side and put a shaggy finger over his mouth.

"Hush ye," it said.

And the boy realized all at once that it was not in fact a creature that had rescued him, but a man. An enormous, ugly, hairy, one-eyed man. A wild man, a *wodewose*.

The boy stopped screaming.

The two sat across from one another on the thick branch in silence while below, the dogs— now equally silenced—circled and circled. The boy was still hot and cold with fright; the wild man's ugly, ridged, scarred face with its bulbous nose and one blind eye did nothing to reassure him. But as the wild man made no move to harm him, the boy finally understood that the wode-wose had, for whatever reasons, risked his own life to rescue him. So at last the boy relaxed. He even tried to smile at the wild man. However, the gapped grin he got in return did not help his sense of dis-ease.

The boy stared down at the circling pack and the dogs returned his stare. There were seven dogs in all, the largest a brindled mastiff, the smallest a stubby-legged rathound. None looked particularly well fed, and the ones with the heavy coats were matted with burrs. He could not tell which one was the leader of the pack, though he guessed it to be the mastiff by its size. He was startled by the liquid shine of their eyes.

Dogs, his conscious mind told him. But as he continued to gaze down, he became mesmerized by them, and suddenly he found himself shoulder to shoulder, nose to nose with the dogs under the shadowy canopy of leaves.

Now he understood it was *not* the mastiff who led the pack, for while it had the mass, it was not particularly intelligent. The leader was a smaller, broad-chested bulldog with large, yellowing teeth.

The dogs looked at him quizzically and sniffed him over: nose, neck, legs, rear. He sniffed them back; their familiar rank smell spoke of hunger and fear/not fear. He found to his surprise that he could read each dog by its stink.

The bulldog lifted its leg against the oak, marking the tree, then turned to speak in a high tenor voice. "Take your place."

The others answered in short, sharp agreement. "Place...place...place."

The boy sang along with them, as if he had no ideas of his own, only the single mind of the pack. "Place!" he cried out.

As if pleased with this response, the bulldog turned its back and started off across the green meadow, the others trailing behind. Soon all the boy could see of them was the swath they had cut through the grass. He took one step after them, then another, blinked, and found himself sitting once more in the oak tree, the wild man across from him.

"Place," the boy whispered.

The wodewose shook his head. "Packs got no reason, lad," he said. "Thee must not run with them. Place be what is wrong with the world." Then he leaped from the tree and headed into the deeper woods.

"Wait!" the boy cried out.

But the wild man was gone.

5. WILD FOLK

HE FOLLOWED THE WODEWOSE FOR SEV-
eral hours, stopping only to gather late bramble-
berries to quiet the rumbling of his stomach. It
was not until nearly the very end of his journey
that he understood that the wild man had left him
a readable trail on purpose: a broken branch here,
a bit of fur caught on briar there, a scuffed foot-
print. As long as he looked carefully, there were
signs.

He had no doubt the wild man could have gone
through the woods leaving no sign at all. He had
heard the stories. How the wodewose lived in the
company of serpents and wolves and the mam-

moth forest bulls. How their strength lay in their shaggy locks which if shorn left them pitiful and weak. How they lived on water and flesh, the water from the streams and the raw flesh of wild beasts. How like kings in their castles, they ruled a great domain, but their vassals were stag and doe, boar and sow, he-bear and she-bear, all the inhabitants of the wood.

As he remembered the tales, he lost the thread of the wild man's trail and stumbled—as if by chance—into another meadow that was small and manageable and ringed by tall beech trees. And there, in tented dwellings, like the Hebrews of old, was an entire town of wild men. And wild women. And wild children as well.

Astonished, he stood for a moment, unmoving.

It was one of the wild children who first spotted him, calling out in a high, thin voice, the accent almost masking meaning, "Look, 'ee, wha' cum 'ere."

Alerted, the rest of the wild folk looked up from their chores. Some had been stretching hides, some cutting great logs, still others turning spitted meat over small cookfires. But at the child's warning—for warning it seemed to be—they stared at the intruder and cried out as with a single voice some kind of wild ululation.

Slowly, hands out to show he meant them no harm, the boy came into their midst and they all arose, ringing him round. The men were in the front, women and children behind.

He tried not to stare at them but could not help himself. They were to a man shaggy, dressed in leather skins and jackets of fur, with unkempt beards and long, straggly locks; their faces were all horribly scarred and scored as if with fire or brands. The women were more civilized looking, their hair less matted, many carefully braided. The skin clothing the women wore was decorated with feathers and quills. One woman, with bright red hair, had even plaited flowers in her hair.

The children were indistinguishable boys from girls in their deerskin clothing and unbound locks. He did not think he could tell any of them apart, except that some were more delicately featured and these he took to be girls. He was to discover later on that this was not always true.

"Where . . . is . . . the . . . one . . . who . . . found . . . me?" he asked, spacing his words out carefully and gesturing broadly, as if talking to an infant or to a person from another land. He was not sure if they could understand his dialect.

A babble of voices surrounded him, their language like water over stone. The children laughed, hiding their mouths behind their hands.

"They laugh at the slowness of thy tongue," came a familiar low voice.

The boy turned and saw the one-eyed wodewose.

"The children laugh at thy clothing, never having seen any like it. Thee art a strange sight to them," the wodewose continued.

The soft laughter came again.

"Never?"

"We keep ourselves to ourselves," the wodewose said, and the adults nodded in agreement. "'Tis better that way. We who are grown have seen too much o' the world outside our woods. War and plague and the branding of those who be taking from the overfull larders of the rich to feed their own starving children. The slander of innocents, the burning of witches, the beating of women. We be having enough o' that."

There was a low murmur that ran around the

circle, a dark complement to the light childish laughter.

The boy nodded.

"Best we bring thee food," the wild man said. "Thee hath made long passage to find us." He started to turn. "Come!" he said, looking over his shoulder.

The crowd broke apart to let the boy through and he followed the wodewose, needing two steps to the wild man's one. He could feel the wild folk behind him staring silently. But one small child, whose white-blond shoulder-length hair fairly glowed in the sunlight, followed right at his heels, crying out, "'Oo be thee? 'Uht be thee?" till he turned suddenly and stared down at the child. With a delighted gasp, the child scampered away and hid behind a tent.

"Do not let our Cub affright thee," the wodewose said.

The boy found that funny and he laughed out loud. "I think rather I affrighted the Cub."

"Aught affrights that one," the wodewose said, but with such affection, the boy wondered if the child were the wild man's own. "'Tis all a game for that one. Dogs, wolves, even bears. He comes home with them, one and all. They follow him and do us no harm. He be growing up a king o' these woods."

"Is that possible?" the boy asked, but in a quiet, respectful voice, because suddenly it seemed to him that with these wild folk anything was possible. Anything at all.

6. BEDDING

DINNER WAS LIKE—AND NOT LIKE—DIN-
ners the boy had had before. Not only did the
wild folk roast spit meat on open fires, but they
cooked leeks and wild garlic, mushrooms and
dark root vegetables in earthenware vessels buried
in the coals. At the end of the meal there was
even a pudding of wild plums flavored—so the
wodewose told him—with sweet cicely. The boy
had not been so full except for dining in Duke
Vortigern's kitchen the one time.

"Do you always eat this way?" he asked.

"This way...that way..." Cub said. He sat
snugged up 'twixt boy and wodewose.

The wodewose laughed, his good eye closing to

a slit. "In wintertide it be sparer. But we know the woods and we know where the food be. We build no stone houses for we must go where needs send. But all the forest be our place." He cuffed Cub good-naturedly; the child giggled at the soft blow and settled under the man's arm.

"Does he stay then?" asked one of the women, pointing to the boy. She had bristly black hair and something like a brand on her cheek.

A second woman, the redhead, added, "Thems that eats, works."

The women set up a babble of agreement until the wild man held up his hand. They silenced at once.

"He be abandoned in the woods," the wodewose said. "He be one of ours."

The black-haired woman spat to one side. "He be too old for abandoning. Like as not he's run off."

"Run away or thrown away," the wodewose said, "he be ours. Can thee honestly say *thee* did not run off?"

The dark-haired woman gave the wodewose an unreadable look and walked away. After a moment, the other women followed her.

The boy was uneasy with what he had just heard. "I do not mean to stay with you more than this one night," he said. "I do not intend to be a..."

"A wild man?" The wodewose laughed, but this time his eye did not become a slit. "Art thee not one already?"

The boy did not answer. He had meant to say he did not intend to be a trouble to them. He feared that his trail might yet lead Fowler to this quiet camp. And if Fowler, why not Vortigern and his men? But the wodewose's question bothered him so much, he knew he would have to give it thought. Once he had, indeed, lived in the woods on his own, thrown away by someone whose face he had never been able to recall, not even in dreams. But this time he was in the woods because he had willed it himself. Was there a difference? And if there was, what should be his response to it?

"Come," the wodewose said, breaking through the boy's reverie. "I will show thee where to sleep the night."

They walked to one of the hide tents and the

wild man gestured to it. "This be the tent for boys. Till thee has a name."

"But I already have a name," the boy said. "Two actually. Hawk. And Hobby." He did not give his true name, Merlin, which was another kind of hawk altogether. For some reason, it suddenly seemed important to him to keep that name hidden.

"Woods name be one thing, town name an other," said the wodewose.

The boy nodded. He had always known names were powerful, so it did not surprise him that the wild man knew it, too.

"Now, Hawk-Hobby, thee must make thy own bed. No one serves an other here. No one rules an other here. As the Greenwitch says, if thee eats with us, thee must work with us."

"What do I make the bed of?" Hawk-Hobby asked. When he had lived in the woods before, he had had no regular bed but had lain in trees for safety, a different tree each night. When he had lived at Master Robin's farm, Mag and Nell had stuffed his mattress with dried grasses and his comforter with feathers from the geese. When he had traveled with the players Ambrosius and Viviane, he had slept in a box bed in their cart. He had actually never made a bed for himself.

"Thy place, thy choice," the wodewose said, holding up the tent flap for the boy to enter. "So thee must choose with care." Then he dropped the flap and was gone.

Looking around the tent, the boy saw there were already several beds—hide pallets actually —but they were clearly spoken for. The imprint of bodies was on them and there were yew bows and arrows by the side of two of the beds, a stick dolly by another. He went over to one of the hides and put his hand inside, drawing out a bit of the bedding. It consisted of dried grasses and was musty smelling; not at all sweet, like Mag's stuffing.

The wodewose was gone and there was no one in the tent to ask, so he lifted up the flap and looked about the camp. There seemed to be only women working for the moment, and frankly they all frightened him.

"I will find something by myself," he murmured. The grass around the camp was all trampled down, and he knew he would prefer something fresh. So he walked to the meadow's edge, listening carefully for a minute in case he should hear again the baying of hounds. Then he plunged into the woods.

There was something resembling a trail and he followed it, noting his surroundings carefully so he did not get lost. Light was still plentiful in the meadow, but the trail through the woods was already grey with the coming night. Fifteen minutes from the camp he came upon another patch of high meadow and, near it, a tangle of flowering marjoram. He had no carry-bag, so he stripped off his shirt, bundling the grasses and spicy herb together.

Never minding that his chest and arms were now goosefleshed with the cold, he hoisted the full shirt-bag and followed the path back to the camp. He was sure the women would be pleased with his energy.

No one paid him any mind when he returned. So he found the boys' tent and went in. When he had dumped his precious grasses into an empty hide mattress, the thing was not even a quarter full.

He had to make five trips in all before he had

the bed full enough to sleep on. By then it was dark, and he was so exhausted he could have slept on the ground. No other boys were yet in the tent, but he was too tired to care. He lay down and fell into a sleep as soft as the bed. His dreams— whatever they were—were as spicy as the herb.

7. QUARRELS

HAWK-HOBBY WOKE TO A LOUD NOISE OUT-side the tent. For a moment he feared that Fowler had found the camp, then realized the voices were all women's. And they were quarreling.

He sat up, leaning on one elbow, and saw that the other beds in the tent were now occupied by five boys near his age, and on another the child, Cub, was curled around the stick dolly. The boys were all laughing silently, hands across their mouths.

"What does it mean?" Hawk-Hobby asked, pointing toward the sound of the women's argument.

"'Ee..." one boy said, his hand barely moving

from his mouth. Then he was convulsed again with silent laughter, and falling back on his bed.

"'Ee..." a second boy added. "They mock 'ee." He, too, collapsed backward with a fit of giggles.

The other boys did not even try to speak, so caught were they by the joke's contagion.

Cub did not laugh. He got off his pallet and came over to Hawk-Hobby, handing him the stick dolly. "Poppet will guard 'ee from the women," he said with great seriousness. Then he went over to the tent flap and lifted it slightly to listen. After a moment, he turned back, "Ooooo, what has 'ee done?"

"I have done nothing," Hawk-Hobby said, suddenly consumed by guilt for all that he actually had done long before he met the wild folk. He stood up and went over to the tent flap to listen. But when he stuck his head out, the women saw him and their indignation rose even louder till the wodewose himself left the cookfire where the men were huddled.

"Na, na," he said, by way of trying to quiet the women. It was only when he held up his hands in mock surrender that they were finally still.

"Come out, boy," he called to Hawk-Hobby.

Hawk-Hobby started out, remembered the stick dolly, and gave it back to the child. "Best keep Poppet from this trouble, whatever it be," he said. He meant it half humorously, but Cub took the dolly and scrambled back onto his bed to store the stick doll there.

"What ails them?" Hawk-Hobby asked, with a lightness he certainly did not feel.

"They be angry with thee," the wodewose said. "It never be wise to anger women."

"But what have I done?" asked Hawk-Hobby. "I have done nothing wrong."

"Wrongness be in the beholder's eye," the wodewose said. "Else we all be innocents indeed." He smiled, but it was not reassuring. "Bring out thy bedding. I cannot go in, for I be a man and that be the boys' tent."

Puzzled, Hawk-Hobby went back and dragged out his bedding, grimly aware that the boys were still laughing at him. But little Cub, at least, tried to help, holding up one end of the hide. That he proved more trouble than help did not matter. Hawk-Hobby gave him a wink by way of thanks and Cub's face immediately lit up.

No sooner was the mattress clear of the tent

flap than the women circled it and began pulling the bedding apart, roughly grabbing out handsful of grass and spreading them on the ground.

"Here, I worked..." Hawk-Hobby began, but was silenced when the black-haired woman with the scar held up some sprigs of grey-tinted marjoram leaves, now almost black.

"Organy!" she cried in triumph, and the women with her set up caterwauling anew and tore apart the rest of his bedding.

"Organy," breathed Cub next to him. "Oooo, that be bad indeed."

The wodewose grabbed Hawk-Hobby by the arm and led him around the side of the tent, away from the angry women. Cub trotted at their heels. "Thy bed," the wodewose said wearily, "be stuffed with a particular herb. *Organy* in the old tongue. It has many virtues: it cures bitings and stingings of venom, it be proof against stuffed lungs or the swounding of the heart. But it never be used for bedding as it be too precious for that."

"I...I did not know," Hawk-Hobby said miserably.

"'Ee did not know," echoed Cub. "'Ee *did* not."

"Hush ye," said the wodewose, "and be about

36

thy own business." He raised his hand and Cub scampered away around the tent, though Hawk-Hobby could see by the child's shadow that he stopped at the corner and was still listening.

"I only wanted it for the sweet smell," Hawk-Hobby explained. Indeed, it was the truth.

"For the sweet smell?" Clearly the wild man was puzzled.

"Sweet herbs for sweet dreams," Hawk-Hobby finished lamely.

"Dreams!" Cub came skipping back around the corner of the tent. "'Ee has dreams. We like dreams."

"I said to be about thy own business, young Cub. Dreams be not the provenance of children." The wodewose's face was dark, as if a shadow had come over it. He turned back to Hawk-Hobby. "Does thee dream?"

"Does not everybody dream?" Hawk-Hobby was reluctant to discuss his magic with the wild man. But—as if a geas, a binding spell, had been laid upon him—he had to answer when asked about it. And answer truthfully. Though he could give those answers aslant.

"There be night dreams . . . and others," the wild

man said. "And I saw thee dream with the dogs yester morn. Why else would I blaze thee a trail here? Still, I be not certain..."

Hawk-Hobby waited. There was nothing to be answered.

"Be thee...a dream-reader?" the wodewose asked carefully.

Just as carefully, Hawk-Hobby replied. "I have been called so."

"And be thee called in truth?"

Hawk-Hobby sighed. There was no getting by that question. "I surely know what my dreams mean. Or at least I often do." It had seemed at first such a small magic, but everyone was so interested in it. It *had* to mean more.

"Ahhh," the wodewose said. Then he turned abruptly and walked around the tent, calling out to the women in his rumble of a voice: "He be a dream-reader. And we without since the last old one died."

"'Ee surely needs Poppet now," said Cub. "I will bring it to 'ee." He disappeared into the tent.

No sooner was the child gone than the women rounded the corner, arguing as they came.

"He be too young," said the redhead.

"Let him prove it," said an older woman, her hair greying at the temples.

"But why would he say..." the wodewose began. But the women would not let him finish. They grabbed up Hawk-Hobby by the arm, three on one side, three on the other, two behind him. They dragged him back to the mattress, now nothing but a flattened hide, and thrust him down.

"Dream," the black-haired woman commanded.

"Dream," they all cried as if with one voice.

"What? Here? Now?"

Their stone faces were his only answers, so he closed his eyes and called for a dream. Any dream.

Of course no dream came.

8. THE LONG WAIT

THEY KEPT HIM ON THE HIDE FOR HOURS, taking turns watching him. It was a warm autumn day and the sun was blazing in an unclouded sky. Whenever he attempted to leave the hide—to get out of the sun or to relieve himself or simply to stand and stretch—the women made menacing noises and threatened him with long sticks. Then he recalled the stories he had heard about the wild women, stories Mag and Nell had told him when he had been a boy in Master Robin's house: how the wild women stole away human children and ate them.

For the first time he was really afraid.

So he tried once again to dream. Closing his

eyes, he thought about pleasanter times with Master Robin or the happy days in Ambrosius' cart. But the more he tried to dream, the wider awake he remained.

The women did not speak to him, nor with one another, while they were on guard. Their aptitude for silence was appalling.

Very well, he thought. *I will match you in this long wait. I will outlast you.* It occurred to him that as long as they waited for him to dream, they would not be eating him.

Opening his eyes, he stared at each woman in turn. Two he was already familiar with: the branded woman and the redhead. They seemed to be the leaders. But soon he found he could distinguish the others as well. In the tales, the wild women were ugly. Mag had said they were covered with bristles and Nell that their black hair was spotted with moss and lichen. But in fact several of the women of this camp were flaxen-haired and none, as far as he could tell, had bristles. As for being ugly, two or three of them were surprisingly good-looking. And the red-head—though she had a tendency to scowl at him, which wrinkled her forehead—was quite beautiful. *Not,* he reminded himself, *as beautiful as Viviane, the lady of the green castle-cart. But close.*

Neither his staring nor his silence seemed to bother the women. Theirs was a genius for long patience. So after a while, Hawk-Hobby forced himself to look down at the ground to avoid their accusing eyes.

Organy, he thought. Even the smell of it would ever after remind him of their stares and the sun beating down on his uncovered head.

On the ground there were hundreds of ants scurrying between the blades of grass. He was startled by their purposefulness in the midst of his own forced idleness.

Ants, his conscious mind told him. But as he continued staring at the hurrying insects, he became mesmerized by them and suddenly he found himself head to abdomen with them as they threaded their way between towering grasses.

The ants were all yellowish-brown and their elbowed feelers swayed before them to a rhythm he could almost grasp. The sound of the many pairs of marching feet was thunderous. Plodding through the arcade of grass, they marched as if a single thread connected them. They sang as one: "Go the track, don't look back. Go the track. Don't look back." The words repeated over and over. It was hypnotic.

He opened his mouth to sing with them, blinked, and found himself once more sitting on the hide. But the song of the ants was still so compelling, he found himself singing it. "Go the track. Don't look back."

He was interrupted by the women crying out: "The Dreamer. The Dreamer is here."

"But..." he tried to say, "that was no dream." However, he did not know *what* it was, so he forced himself to silence. If the women thought him this Dreamer, and that got him off the hide, allowed him to stretch his legs, or relieve himself, he would agree to anything.

He thought he had been on the hide for hours and hours but when he looked up at the sun, it was not quite noon.

9. DREAMER

THEY FED HIM THEN, EVEN MORE THAN they had at dinner, a strange porridge and a stew that left an odd aftertaste. They made him eat every bite.

He ate steadily and then, when he thought he could not eat anything more, they brought him a sweet honey drink which they insisted he finish. He tried to turn it down but they would not let him. To silence them, he drank it all. At last, with aching, taut belly, he tried to stand and found his legs would not hold him up.

"I feel..." he began, not knowing what he was feeling. And turning his head to one side, he was suddenly and quite efficiently sick.

When he was done, the women helped him stand and guided him to a place somewhere on the edge of the camp. Through slotted eyes he tried to make it out, but could not. His head was swimming about and he was afraid he might be sick again.

"This be thy place now," the black-haired woman with the cheek brand was saying, her voice remarkably similar to the bulldog's.

Place. That was good, he thought drowsily. He needed a place.

The woman gave him a little push in the small of his back and he fell, rather than walked, into it.

The place was small and dark and closely covered. There was some sort of mattress, thin and old smelling. He did not care. He curled up on it and fell instantly to sleep.

This time he dreamed.

He dreamed of the bear again, but now he was in the dream as well, holding a sword in one hand, a large stone in the other. The bear took off its crown and flung it onto the sword. At that, sword and crown dissolved and he woke sweating and ill.

It did not help that his small, closed-in tent seemed to be swaying. It did not help that the air stank of his sickness. He tried to get to his feet and banged his shoulder painfully against something. His head hurt. His belly ached. The slightest noise hammered at his temples like a blacksmith's hammer on an anvil.

Heavily he fell again onto his pallet where he slept, dreamed, woke, slept again. The dream images all blended into one great dream of kings and kingdoms.

Suddenly an enormous light—like the light of heaven itself—flooded into his dream. He opened his eyes and found that he was lying in an open space. The tent had been lifted away and the light was the new day.

Only then did he see what his *place* really was. He was in some sort of large wicker cage hanging from a tree limb some five feet off the ground. When he tried the cage door, it would not open. Not that this was exactly a surprise. It was tied shut with a complicated knot on the outside that he could not reach, no matter how hard he tried.

A cage. Like a criminal hung up at the crossroads to starve. Or like the sacrifice of the Druid priests.

"Or like," he whispered to himself, "a beast in a trap." He thought wildly: *They are fattening me for a feast.*

He gazed about. He seemed to be alone. Once more he tried to reach the knot, straining his arm as far as it could go. He could touch it . . . but just. There was no way he could get it untied. *What a fool I have been,* he thought. *Stuffing myself when I should have been starving.* He sat back down heavily on the pallet. The movement caused the cage to sway and his stomach to heave.

"Dreamer!" A woman's voice called and reluctantly he looked toward the sound. It was the redheaded woman. How could he ever have thought such a witch beautiful? "Dreamer!" Her voice made his head ache the more. "Here be herbs for thy sickness. For thy stomach, cuckoo's meat; it will strengthen thy belly and procure thy appetite. And this other . . ." she pointed to a smaller vessel, "bruisewort. That thee must sniff up into thy nostrils and it will purge thy head. We apologize for the ruse. But it be necessary to take thee, unprotesting, to thy place."

47

"Go away, witch," he mumbled. His own voice hurt his head as well.

"Once thy sickness be gone, we will hear thy dreams."

"I will take nothing from your hands. Nothing. I will starve myself before I take something from you. Then what kind of a meal will I make?" It was, he thought, a strong speech. That was why he was stunned when she began to laugh. It was a pretty laugh, soft, tinkling.

"Eat thee? Eat another human soul? What does thee take us for?"

Was this a trick? He could not think, his head hurt so.

"All we want from thee are thy dreams. Come, take these herbals. They will cure what ails thee." She held out the vessels again.

He did not have the will to argue longer. *And,* he reminded himself, *to escape he would need a clear head.*

"Give them here," he said, and she put the vessels into his hand. He took the stuff as ordered, drinking the one, sniffing the other, which made him sneeze five times in a row. The sneezing did not help his hurting head.

But within the hour, almost miraculously, felt quite bright-headed, and his stomach no longer ached. This time when he looked out from the cage, the scene below him took on a serene beauty. The wild men were stretching hide skins between saplings; the women, in a cluster, pushed bone needles through deerskin, gossiping happily. Throughout the camp the children played games that he recognized: beggar-thy-neighbor, leap-frogs, hide-then-seek, and tag.

It looked like any country village. Like a home.

Except ... he thought ... except their houses were tents, there were no streets, and he was stuck up in a wicker cage, suspended in the air, while his captors were waited for him to read his dreams.

What else they might want of him, should his dreaming fail, he was too afraid to ask.

10. DREAM CAGE

HE HAD NO IDEA HOW MANY DAYS HE RE-
mained in the cage. He tried to keep them sep-
arate in his mind, but they tended to run together.
Each time he woke, the women gave him an
herbal draught, then listened to his latest dreams.
He never lied about the dreams, nor made one
up. Indeed, he could not have, even had he
wanted to.

He dreamed of a table round as a wheel that
rolled across the land leaving great wide ruts. He
dreamed of huge stones walking across the ocean.
He dreamed of a giant, green as May, who threw
his head in the air like a child with a ball. He
dreamed of a man and a woman asleep in one

bed, a sword between them sharper than any desire.

He told the wild women all these dreams.

At each telling, they listened politely, then debated among themselves the meanings of the dreams. The table, they said, was the year, sometimes winter and sometimes summer. The stones, they said, were the Saxon army come across the sea. The giant, they said, was the Green Man come to save them. The man and woman and sword, they said, were of no consequence, having naught to do with them, but with the nobles in their fancy houses.

They never asked him what he thought of the dreams, and here they erred. For they were mistaken in every particular about the dreams, this he knew. The dreams were each a slantwise reading of his own future. He was sure of it. They had nothing to do with the wild folk at all.

None of the men or children came near the cage. Dreaming, it seemed, was the provenance of women. None, that is, but the child Cub, who stood back a ways to be able to see into the cage, but did not speak. It was not that the child was shy, lest he had been made shy by Hawk-Hobby's elevation to Dreamer. But the distance he had to stand made conversation awkward. He was only a small child, after all.

One morning—perhaps it was the third or fourth—desperate for information or even a more human encounter, Hawk-Hobby called out to the child: "How is that Poppet of yours?"

Cub opened his mouth to answer, thought better of it, and scampered away. But he appeared again soon after with the dolly in hand. Throwing it with careful aim up into the cage, he cried out, "Poppet will guard 'ee." Then he ran off again and this time did not come back.

"Poppet didn't do such a good job last time," Hawk-Hobby mused, but he kept the doll, tucked up under his pallet. Indeed, the child did not come close again so he could not return the toy.

A day or so later, when he had been taken from the cage by the women to cleanse himself in a nearby stream, he suddenly realized why he had had trouble counting off the days in the cage.

"They have put something in my food," he whispered to himself. "Something to make me sleep.

Something to encourage me to dream." The sound of the river hid his words from the wild women guarding him on the shore.

He wondered that it had taken him so long to figure it out, then guessed that the draughts themselves had kept him from the knowledge. He realized, too, that *anyone* so drugged would dream. "Which is why," he whispered, "the wild folk would ordinarily only use the old ones, the ones past hunting or harvesting. The old ones whose bones are too brittle to carry them through the woods. It would be a mercy, really, for them to be so employed; a mercy to dream away the tag ends of their lives." He remembered how surprised they had been that he admitted to being a dreamer.

But, he thought, *I am a dreamer even without the draughts.* And for the first time he wondered —really wondered—what good this dreaming was to him. As a warning, a dream was all but useless if it could not be properly read. How was he to learn, beyond his instinctive guesses, the language of his dreams? Who was he to tell what he discovered therein? Such dreams might guide kings and kingdoms. Such dreams might prophesy the movements of armies. Such dreams might direct the marriage of princes, the death of queens, and the birth of royal babes. But what good were they here in the wild amongst the wodewose?

"And what good are they," he said to himself, "in the hands of a boy like me?"

He was still puzzling it out when they returned him to the wicker cage. He refused to eat or drink. "I do not need this to dream," he told them.

They did not believe him. But they no longer had the power to compel.

They brought him food in the small clay bowls and he refused it all. For two days he was the captive of bad dreams.

He slept curled over an aching belly, Poppet clutched in his arms. He woke sweating and hollow. He shook. He shivered. His bones felt like fire, then ice. Many times he was on the verge of crying out for one of the draughts. But Poppet would caution him in Cub's voice. "Do not rise to the lure," the dolly said. "This is *not* your place. Go the track. Don't look back." In his true waking moments he knew that Poppet did not talk. But deep in his dreams he was not so sure.

"Dreamer," other voices, women's voices, cozzened him. "Eat. Drink. This will cure what ails thee." But he continued to resist, saying, "I do not need that to dream. I do not need that to dream."

The women did not believe him, of course, but they watched as his body cleansed itself of all their herbs. And when he finally sat up without shaking, the only one to see him was Cub, who watched silent and still.

"Here," Hawk-Hobby called to the child. "Take Poppet. It has guarded me well. Now it must guard you."

The child shook his head, but came over anyway and Hawk-Hobby held the doll out to him.

The moment Cub's hand touched the dolly, something odd and wild and strange seemed to bond them. It was as if a spark of lightning shot from one hand, through the poppet, to the other.

And Hawk-Hobby dreamed.

He dreamed that in the meadow a fountain of blood burst through the grass. It covered the feet of the wild folk, rose to their ankles, kept rising till it covered their shoulders, necks, heads. They cried out for help, but there was no sound. And Poppet alone escaped, sailing over the river of blood in the wicker cage, the sails powered by its own breath.

It was his first dream about the wild folk themselves.

And his last.

11. MAGIC

IT WAS AN AWFUL DREAM. TERRIBLE. HE woke from it screaming.

Cub grabbed Poppet and stumbled back from the force of the scream, then turned and ran screaming himself into the midst of the women.

Hawk-Hobby could not hear what the child said. He was too far away for that. But clearly whatever Cub said startled the women, shocking them into action. They all came toward the cage at a run, and the men—a bit more tentatively—behind them.

"What was thy dream, Dreamer?" the black-haired woman asked.

He told it all: the meadow, the blood, the doll, the boat, the breath.

There was much consternation among them as they discussed the dream. Though they did not ask him what it meant, much they could read on their own. The meadow filled with blood was too obvious to ignore. Arguments over, they turned as one to begin the work of packing up the camp.

"Ask me," he called after them. He thought he knew more than they had found in the dream. He was, himself, the doll; a toy in the wrong hands, a magic creature in the right. With his breath he could work magic. Magic more powerful than the spilling of blood. Surely *that* is what the dream meant. But someone needed to ask before he could answer. He understood that much about his ability to read dreams.

It was as though they had forgotten him completely. They were much too busy with their move. Striking the tents, the men rolled them into tight bundles. The women covered the campfires with dirt, then sorted through the drying herbs and strips of meat. Even the children worked, placing clothes and other small belongings into packs. If they all seemed to agree on one thing, it was that the meadow was a place of coming destruction. Blood. They were best gone from it. And quickly.

Only Cub was oblivious to the activity, intent, instead, on something on the ground.

From so far away Hawk-Hobby could not see what fascinated the child. But when a woman, noticing the idle child, cuffed him roughly, both Cub and Hawk-Hobby cried out at the same time: Cub because his ear rang with the blow and the caged Dreamer because his own ear ached in sympathy, as if he and the child were now one.

Cub turned slowly at the sound of the Dreamer's voice, his hand still cupped over his aching ear. Then his face lit up and he bent down to pick up the thing from the ground. Running over, he smiled up at Hawk-Hobby. There were streaks on his cheeks where tears had run down but he was no longer crying.

"Look!" he said, holding up a grubby hand. There was a robin in his open palm, its head hanging to one side as if its neck were broken. "Make robin sing, Dreamer. Make robin fly."

Hawk-Hobby took the bird without hesitation, not quite knowing why. The child's request was gentle enough. More a plea than a demand. But for some reason it seemed as strong as a geas, a magic compulsion. He took the bird and looked down at it. Its orange breast was already dulled in death and there was not so much as a murmur beneath its feathers. Its eyes were cloudy and its little feet stiff.

"'Ee must fix it, Dreamer," the child said.

"And you must get me Poppet. To guard the bird," Hawk-Hobby said. He said it more to gain time than because he thought it might be any help.

The child ran off to fetch his dolly. Hawk-Hobby sat down in the cage, his legs swinging over the side. He remembered the magician Ambrosius bringing flowers out of his sleeves and coins from behind a man's ear. Such magicks, he had soon found out, were but sleights of hand. One needed to have flowers up one's sleeve to bring them down. One needed a coin hid in the palm to make it appear at a man's ear. What the child was asking of him was more than that, was the very breath of life.

Breath.

That was one component of the dream. The

poppet's breath powering the sails of the wicker boat.

He brought the little bird up even with his face. Close it was even more pathetic, already cooling. Parting its beak with two careful fingers and then closing his eyes, he remembered the exact feeling in the dream and blew three short breaths into the bird. They were small breaths—of air, of life. He did not know what else to do.

For a long moment nothing happened. Nothing at all. Except that the clearing and the woods stilled around him.

Then, as if a light had come down from heaven, piercing his head, and a second light had come up from earth, through his feet, he was shot through with a great energy. Between his palms the bird began to warm. A small flutter started beneath the flame-colored breast. The legs twitched, so hard one of the tiny nails on its feet scratched his finger.

"Tic!" the bird said suddenly, sharply. "Tic!" Then it poured out the clear jangling warble of its autumn song.

Stunned—but not really surprised—Hawk-Hobby threw the bird into the open air where it shook its wings and, still singing, flew off into the sky.

Exhausted by his first real magic, Hawk-Hobby sank back onto the hide pallet, suddenly too tired to do more.

12. FREEDOM

TWO PEOPLE—AND TWO ONLY—HAD SEEN
what happened. Cub had crept back, dolly in
hand, and watched as the robin lifted off the boy's
sweaty palm and flung itself into the lightening
air. The other watcher was the wodewose himself,
standing to one side, his good eye blinking as if
not quite crediting what he had seen.

"Surely," the man said to himself, "thee be
much more than a dreamer." He left the hide he
had been packing and strode over to the cage.

"Who art thee?" he demanded. "What art thee?"

"He is Dreamer," the child said, satisfied. "He
is Breath of Dream. He is Maker."

The wodewose paid the child no attention. "What art thee?" he asked again.

"I am a boy," Hawk-Hobby answered carefully, but the magic demanded more of him now. A direct answer to a direct question. "I am..." And suddenly he realized he did not know *what* he was any longer. Boy. Man. Mage. In one brilliant light-filled moment he had been changed beyond all recognition.

What am I indeed? he wondered. *A magician full of tricks and misdirections like Ambrosius? Or a wizard in truth?* He had made a dead bird fly. *Perhaps...* he thought recklessly, *perhaps I am a god. Or a demon.* Vaguely he recalled, as if it had been a dream, someone calling him that. *What am I indeed?*

"I am...an orphan," he said at last. That much he was sure of. "I am alone."

"We take orphans," the wodewose said. "They be our children."

"Take?"

"From hillsides where they be abandoned. From villages where they be abused. From cradles where they be forgotten." There was a kind of mercy in his one good eye. As he spoke his ugly face took on a rough beauty. "We only take what is not wanted."

"As you took me," Hawk-Hobby pointed out. "From the dogs."

The eye suddenly turned crafty. "But did thee run *from* the dogs, or did thee run *with* them?"

Remembering for a moment how he *had* been part of the pack, Hawk-Hobby was silent.

"What art thee?" the wodewose asked again. "Be thee Green Man? Be thee Robin o' the Wood? What hath thee been called?"

"I have been called many things," the boy answered honestly. "I told you that before. I have been called Hawk. I have been called Hobby." He took a breath, remembering the falconer who had found him in the woods and became his first father. Master Robin. He saw suddenly how he could honor the man and remain truthful. "Robin is as good a name as any."

"Hah!" the wodewose exclaimed. "Thee made the robin live again, so thee may be Robin indeed. Be thee merciful to us, Robin." He made a sketchy bob with his head, then his eye suddenly scrunched up. "But Robin o' the Woods is a tricksy spirit. I must think more on this." So saying, he left, walking out into the meadow and leaving the others to their mundane tasks.

But Cub stayed behind. "Be 'ee Robin indeed?" he asked, his eyes wide.

"What is a name," Hawk-Hobby asked, "but the outward dressing of a man?"

"The Green Man must not be caged," the child said. "Robin belongs to all the woods."

"Then open the knot, and let me free."

"I cannot reach it," the child said.

"Get me a knife."

"I have none."

It was an impasse and Hawk-Hobby could not think what to do next, but the child had his own ideas.

"If 'ee be Robin indeed, knots cannot bind 'ee."

"Oh, Cub..." Hawk-Hobby began, his voice sounding a hopeless note. But then he thought, *Why not? How much more difficult was it to make a bird fly?* "Hand me your poppet."

With a sudden rush of courage, the child handed up the dolly, as if expecting to receive another shock and prepared to accept it. But this time there was none.

Hawk-Hobby took the doll and stared at it. Then he held it between his palms and breathed three careful breaths onto its berryjuice mouth. Was it his imagination, or did the stick figure move, ever so slightly, in his hands? He stretched full down on the cage bottom and stuck his hand—with the dolly—as far out of the cage as he could. "Is Poppet near the knot?" he called.

"Down more. And more. There!" The child's voice was full of awe.

"All right, Poppet," Hawk-Hobby said, "do thy will." He held onto the head of the doll and with its stick legs poked at the knot. He could not tell if the dolly moved of its own or if his own manipulations did the work, but suddenly Cub cried out, "There! 'Ee's got it!" and the knot came undone.

The child danced up and down, clapping his hand. "Oh, Green Man, 'ee be free. Free."

He did not take time to argue, but swung the door to the cage wide. It was but a quick jump to the ground and but ten steps to the line of trees. He could hear the women's cries behind him and Cub's singular squawl: "Robin, wait for me!"

But he waited for no one as he ran, ever faster, into the woods.

13. HIDING PLACE

HAWK-HOBBY MADE A PATH WHERE NO path had been, dodging through the undergrowth as if the Gabriel hounds, the dogs of hell, were on his trail. And indeed, the women's ululations sounded like the baying of a pack.

But at last he tired of running and made the assumption that no one was following because he no longer could hear the voices, except as a thin honking. Looking up to discover the hour through the trees, he saw a vee of geese heading south, and laughed. Hounds, women, geese—they all sounded the same. Mostly, he told himself, he had been running from his own fear.

He turned to his right and all but fell out onto

a track. It was not a thin path such as a deer and its mate might make, nor the higher broken branches of a bear. It was a true road through the woods, the kind a marching army might take.

He shuddered, remembering his dream, then heard a thrashing and crashing behind him. As startled as any wild thing, he glanced back over his shoulder and prepared himself for a second flight.

"Ro...bin..." came the breathy little voice.

"Oh, Cub, you should have stayed with your family," Hawk-Hobby said, and he went to where the child was struggling through the brush. Picking him up he swung the child onto his shoulders.

"'Ee be my family," the child said. "I have taken 'ee as my own."

"You cannot take me..." Hawk-Hobby began, but the child interrupted.

"Silly Robin. Of course I can. We take who is abandoned. We take what is alone. 'Ee said thou wert alone. I take 'ee."

Hawk-Hobby reached up and set the child back down on the ground. He knelt so they were face to face. "They will worry about you. I must bring you back."

"They will put 'ee in the cage again," Cub said.

Hawk-Hobby shrugged. He would have to deal with that after. But first...

"Hush," the child said. "Listen."

But he had already heard. This time it was the baying of hounds in truth as well as the breathy intake of horses. Somewhere up ahead on the track there was a troop on its way. Neither he nor the child believed it was the wild folk.

"What do we do, Robin?" Cub whispered, slipping his hand with the dolly into Hawk-Hobby's. "Will they take us? Will they hurt us?"

"We dare not run, for the dogs will follow and catch us. We must hide."

They faded back into the undergrowth and searched until they found a sturdy oak well away from the path. Hawk-Hobby boosted the child up into the tree crotch then scrambled up quickly behind him. Then alternately pushing and pulling, he got Cub up into the highest branches where they could lie hidden behind the yellowing leaves.

"Pull your legs to your chest like this," he whispered to the child. "Make yourself small. Make yourself invisible."

The child nodded and did as he was instructed.

They lay still but Hawk-Hobby could see that the branch on which the child huddled trembled. *Magic,* he thought frantically. *Now is when I could really use it.* By this he did not mean the breath of life, the moving poppet, the dreams. What good were they to him in this peril? If he could only call down lightning or call up demons or...

And as he was thinking this, a host of horsemen trotted into view. From the treetop he could catch glimpses of them as they rode, two abreast, their armor dusted with the miles. He could see they wore white plumes and had white dragons embossed on their banners and that told him at once who they were: the soldiers he had dreamed of back in the days when he had lived in the green cart. They were the soldiers he had warned Duke Vortigern against. But Duke Vortigern had not believed him, had thrown him out of the castle, out of the town. Hawk-Hobby took some satisfaction in being right.

But only for a moment.

Duke Vortigern had not believed him. But Fowler had. *Fowler!* No sooner had he thought the name than—as if by magic conjuration—the man himself appeared, walking by the side of the horsemen, his massive dog Ranger held fast on a lead.

"I be frightened, Robin," the child whispered.

Hawk-Hobby put a finger to his mouth to shush the boy. "Be like a deer," he whispered back. "Disappear into stillness."

Cub seemed to understand and, like a fawn in danger, he drew back into the tree and all but vanished.

But the dog had caught the sound or their scent. He sniffed the air, gave tentative tongue.

"Hush, dog," Fowler cried out, but he looked where the dog looked. Then he pointed.

The soldiers halted and the man at the lead turned his horse aside and rode over to Fowler and the dog. "What is it, man? What does that hellhound of yours see?"

The dog pulled his master off the track and into the brush, through nettle and bracken and the brittle brown fern. He circled the oak, barking impatiently.

Fowler stared up into the tree, trying to make

out what the dog was barking at. Shaking his bowstring-colored hair out of his eyes, he peered carefully.

Hawk-Hobby closed his eyes and thought about magic. Thought about it as hard as he could.

The dog suddenly went quiet.

"Well?" called the man on the horse.

Fowler, looking up, saw a shimmer of green behind the yellow leaves, as if some bit of sun had pierced the dark canopy, but nothing more. Whatever had irritated the dog was invisible to the eye. "Nothing, my lord Uther. The dog barks at shadows." He stroked his sparse moustache.

"Then we go on," Lord Uther said. "My men are tired and angry after the battle at Carmar then. That bloody Vortigern burned up with all his possessions. These men fight for so little reward and they sorely miss the spoils they were promised. Shut up that hound of yours and let us be out of this woods. There is dark magic here. Some tricksy Green Man magic. I do not like such conjurations. I do not fight shades."

"Yes, my lord," Fowler said, hauling the dog away.

The horseman spun back to the head of his column of soldiers and they went on. It was nearly dark when the last of them was out of sight.

And darker still when the boy and the child dared to climb down from the tree.

14. BATTLEGROUND

"WHERE DO THEY GO, ROBIN?" THE CHILD asked when they were, at last, on solid ground. He asked—but there was already an uncomfortable certainty in his voice. Cub knew—as Hawk-Hobby guessed—that the track led right back to the wodewose camp.

Hawk-Hobby despaired. They had no way of warning the wild folk. Except, of course, he had warned them already with his dream. He only hoped they had been able to escape in time. An angry, tired army would make quick work of them. Not that he had any love for the wild folk. Except for this yellow-haired child, except for the wodewose himself, they had not been good to him. He wanted to be shed of them but he did not wish them dead. Having recently buried Master Robin, Mag, and Nell, he desired only to be done with death.

"We will go softly, quietly, like a fox, like a wolf, back to the camp," he said.

"I can be a fox," Cub said. "I can be a wolf,"

"I know you can," Hawk-Hobby said. "And we will find everyone well and hale. You will see." He patted the child on the head, thinking to himself that he would see Cub back to his family and make his own escape. Having done it once, he was confident he could do it again. But they were no sooner several steps along the track when there was suddenly thunder, great rolling clanging walls of it, and rain bolted down from the sky.

"Robin, I be afraid." The child clutched his hand tightly and shivered with the wet and cold.

Despite his growing magic, Hawk-Hobby was frightened, too. He was, after all, but twelve years old himself. But he would not let the child see his fear. "Come," he said, "we will not stay out in the storm. Let us shelter in the tree."

"Oh, no, Robin," the child said. "Lightning will hurt us there. We must find a cave."

Hawk-Hobby smiled down at him. "Who knows what beast lives in a cave?"

"Thou art Robin o' the Wood," the child said. "No beast be harming 'ee."

"I have no answer for you that will suffice," Hawk-Hobby said. "We will find a cave." And no sooner had he spoken than—as if by magic—they came upon a cave in a cliffside. It was really more a shelf than a cave, too narrow for a beast's den but wide enough to keep them from the rain. Hawk-Hobby went in first and pulled the child in after. And there, huddled together for warmth, they spent a disquieted night.

The track they followed back to the camp had been well widened by the army. Great swaths of bracken had been crushed beneath the horses' hooves; autumn wildflowers had been ground into the dirt.

The child seemed undismayed by the destruction, set as he was on getting to the camp. But at each step, Hawk-Hobby grew colder and colder. It was not fear he was feeling, but dread. It trickled down like sweat between his shoulder blades.

The child stopped suddenly. "Robin. Listen."

Hawk-Hobby listened. He could hear nothing. And then—as if in another dream—he realized: he could hear *nothing*. No birds, no chirruping insects, not even the grunt and moan of trees as they shifted in their roots. *Nothing*.

"Nothing," he said.

"Robin...I want..." and then Cub began to wail, a sound so alien in the woods that it sent a terrible shiver down Hawk-Hobby's spine.

He gathered the child up in his arms and soothed him until the tears stopped. "Come," he said. "I will hold thee." The deliberate use of the word *thee* had a salutary effect on the child.

"Thee must take *me* now," Cub said.

The track took a slow turning and then they were in the meadow ringed with beech trees. Not a blade of grass stirred between the bodies. The busy, scurrying ants were gone.

The oddest thing, he thought, *is that there is not much blood. Not a flood of it. Not a meadowful.* Just bodies strewn about as though they were dollies flung down by a careless child.

They found the dark-haired scar-faced woman first, lying on her back, her arms spread wide as if welcoming her death. Near her were two of the boys, side by side. Close by them, a third boy and one of the wild men.

He held the child against his shoulder. "Do not look," he cautioned, though he knew from the rigid body that the child was taking it all in. "Do not look."

He wandered across the field of death until he heard an awful sound. It was a dog howling, the cry long and low. He wondered that he had not heard it before. Following the thread of it, he came to the meadow's edge and there was the wodewose and, with him, Fowler. They were locked in an awful embrace. It was Fowler's dog, Ranger, who was howling, his muzzle muddied with blood. When he saw the boys, he shut up and lay down miserably, head on paws, following their every movement with liquid eyes.

"Stay, Ranger," Hawk-Hobby said, trying to put iron in his command.

The dog did not move toward them and, after a minute, Hawk-Hobby put the child down, and examined the dead men.

It was clear to see how it had happened. The wodewose's hands were tightly wrapped around

Fowler's neck, so tightly the traitor's eyes bulged and his tongue protruded from his mouth. Out of the wild man's back stuck the haft of a soldier's spear, and around that wound were bite marks. Which of the two of them had died first hardly mattered.

"Make him live, Dreamer," the child whispered. "Make him live."

Hawk-Hobby took the wodewose by the shoulder and brought the ruined head close to his own. The wild man was stiff with death, his lips parted in a final agony. It was all the boy could do to touch him.

"Give him breath, Dreamer," the child whispered again.

Bending over, though he shook with the horror of it, Hawk-Hobby blew the breath of life into the grimace of a mouth.

Once, twice, three times he blew. Then waited. Then blew again.

He closed his eyes and remembered his dream of breath, remembered how it had felt when he had given life to the little bird. He prayed, sudden tears running down his cheeks.

He blew again.

And again.

And nothing happened.

Nothing at all.

"Make him live, Dreamer," the child begged.

Let him live, the boy prayed.

But his magic—capricious, wanton, unpredict-
able—did not come at his calling.

15. FAMILY

HOW LONG THEY SAT THERE BY THE DEAD men, Hawk-Hobby did not know. But eventually the dog came over to him and licked his hand several times as if learning the taste.

The boy stood. "Come," he said. "It is time for us to go." And the three of them—boy, child, dog—walked together to the edge of the meadow, leaving the dead behind.

"Why did he not live?" Cub asked.

Hawk-Hobby shook his head. "I do not know," he said. "I do not know near enough yet. But I will learn." He looked into the child's face, now streaked with dirt and tears. "I promise you I will learn."

"I will learn, too," the child said to him confidently. "And 'ee will teach me."

They went down the path, but in the opposite direction than the soldiers had taken. The dog ranged ahead, then returned, over and over and over again, as if to satisfy himself the two were safe.

They did not stop until the sun was well overhead.

In a little glade, where berries grew in profusion, they had a meal. In between one juicy handful and the next, Cub turned to the boy. "Are thee my father now?" he asked.

Startled, Hawk-Hobby smiled slowly. The idea was new to him. All this while he had been seeking a father for himself. Now, it seemed, he had a son. "If you wish it."

In answer, the child put his hand in the boy's.

"Then perhaps," Hawk-Hobby said, "if we are to be a family, we need to tell one another our true names."

"But—'ee are Dreamer," the child said. "Robin o' the Wood."

"No," the boy answered, kneeling before the child. "I am a dreamer, true, but that is not my true name. My name..." He took a deep breath. "My name is Merlin."

"Like the hawk?" the child asked. "I like hawks."

"Like the hawk. And someday I shall teach you how to tame them as I was taught," Merlin said. "But now I have many other things to teach you. Such as what your place is in this world. And that you must not rise to the lure. And..."

"But *my* name, Merlin. What be 'ee calling me?"

"Cub."

"Can I be bigger than a cub?"

"You will be in time."

"As big as...as big as a bear? Then no one could kill what is mine. If I be big and powerful as a bear."

Merlin smiled. "As big as a bear, certainly," he said. "But if you are a bear, Cub, then we shall call you Artus, for that means bear-man." As he said it, he suddenly remembered his dream of the bear. Perhaps, perhaps this was meant, after all.

"Artus. Artus. Artus," the child cried out, twirling around and around until he was quite dizzy with it.

At the sound of the child's name, the dog burst out of the woods and ran about the two of them, barking.

"Ranger," commanded Merlin, "do your duty to this King Bear."

Inexplicably, the dog stopped and bowed its head. Then, when Artus laughed delightedly, and clapped his berry-stained hands, the dog turned and ran back down the path as if to scout the long, perilous way.

Light.

Morn.

"How can I continue, how can I rule now that he is gone?"

"You are king, my lord. He was just an old mage. And he lacked all humility."

"Hush. He was my father. He was my teacher. He was my friend."

"A king has no friends, my lord."

"Not even you, Gwen?"

"Not even me, Arthur."

"You are wrong, you know. He was my friend from the first moment I saw him. Though I did not

know then—or ever—what he truly was. Sometimes he seemed to me to be as fierce as a wild dog, sometimes as busy as an ant, ofttimes as slippery as a trout. He was a hawk, a hobby, a merlin."

"He was a man, my lord."

"Not a man like me, Gwen."

"No one is like you, Arthur."

"No one?"

"You are the king."

"So am I powerful?"

"Very powerful."

"That is good. If I am powerful, then no one can hurt me. Or mine. So why do I hurt so now that he is gone?"

And he calls his servants to him with a bell that sounds like a tamed hawk's jesses, like the sound of spears clashing on earth, that place perilously juxtaposed between heaven and hell.

AUTHOR'S NOTE

The story of Merlin, King Arthur's great court magician, is not one story but many. Tales about him have been told in England, in Scotland, in Ireland, in Wales, in Brittany, France, Germany, and beyond. In some of the stories he is a Druid priest, in others a dream-reader, a shape-shifter, a wild man in the woods.

In Geoffrey of Monmouth's twelfth-century *Vita Merlini*—*The Life of Merlin*—the great magician goes insane and runs off into the woods for a while where he lives as a wild man and only music can soothe him.

Wild men were popular figures in medieval literature and art. Known also as wodewose, they were sung about in French romances, found in sophisticated paintings, woven into enormous tapestries, carved onto ornamented weapons. There was even a famous set of fifteenth-century German playing cards that had a suit called "wild men." But the wold man or wild man was outside of the strictly ordered medieval society, a kind of jester, preternaturally wise. Often he became mixed up in the folk mind with the ancient gods of the woods: Silvanus, the Green Man, Robin o' the Wood, Robin Hood.

In the old stories of Merlin and Arthur, Merlin's roles were various. In some he was there at Arthur's conception, helping Arthur's father, Uther Pendragon, and Arthur's mother, Ygraine, get together by supernatural means. In other stories he is Arthur's teacher, patient and wise. In others he is the architect of Arthur's Camelot, of Stonehenge, of the round table. In all, he is a figure of magic, of mystery, his own history beguiling, a fatherless (and perhaps even motherless) figure who helps raise Arthur the child.

I have taken bits and pieces of these stories, reworked them extensively, and added to them information about the wodewose societies where

the men were often pictured as one-eyed mon-
sters (like the Greek Cyclops) dressed in bear-
skins with shaggy, bristly, ugly wives. That there
were outlaw groups living in the vast forests of
old Britain, we know. Whether Merlin—boy or
man—ever encountered any such is the realm of
the storyteller.

—J. Y.